Trapper's Guide to Greek Mythology

Trapper Stocks

Opal Kingdom Press

Dedicated to my good friends Hadlee, Sullivan, and Sam

Contents

Chapter 1

Introduction to Greek Mythology

G reek mythology is the stories created and shared by the ancient people of Greece. They are a rich tapestry of stories of gods, heroes, and strange creatures that have captivated imaginations for centuries. These ancient tales originated in the culture of ancient Greece and have endured through the ages, shaping literature, art, and even modern-day language and thought. I fell in love with Greek Mythology after reading the Percy Jackson books by Rick Riordan and wanted to learn more about the real myths. I did a lot of reading and research and put together this guide! I hope through this guide you will learn to love them too.

What is Greek Mythology?

At its core, Greek mythology consists of a collection of stories and beliefs passed down orally – that means people telling other people - through generations of Greeks. These myths served multiple purposes in ancient Greek society: a way to explain natural phenomena, understand the workings of the world, and explore fundamental questions about human nature, mortality, and the divine. Over time these myths were shared with the rest of the world, both by word of mouth and by being written down and shared.

Origins and Development of Greek Mythology

The origins of Greek mythology are shrouded in the mists of time, stretching back to the earliest civilizations of the Aegean Bronze Age. Many of the myths we know today were first recounted in the works of ancient Greek poets and writers, such as Homer, Hesiod, and the playwrights of classical Athens, but we're not sure if these writers first made the myths up, or gathered them from other sources.

Over time, Greek mythology evolved and adapted, influenced by contact with other cultures, shifts in political power, and the changing beliefs and values of Greek society. Despite these changes, the core themes and characters of Greek mythology remained constant, providing a shared cultural framework for the people of ancient Greece.

The Importance of Myth in Ancient Greece

Myth played a central role in ancient Greek society, permeating every aspect of life from religion and politics to art and literature. The gods and heroes of Greek mythology were not distant deities but active participants in the lives of mortals, intervening in human affairs, inspiring works of art and literature, and serving as moral and cultural examples and warnings. If you were good and obedient you might be able to be a hero, but if you were bad then you might just get eaten by a terrible monster.

The myths of ancient Greece were also a source of entertainment and education, providing a lot of rich material for poets, playwrights, and storytellers to draw upon. Retellings and performances of the myths were often a central part of public festivals and religious ceremonies, reinforcing social cohesion and shared cultural identity.

Moreover, Greek mythology served as a way for the Greek people to make sense of the world and their place within it, offering explanations for natural phenomena, the origins of humanity, and the mysteries of life and death. By exploring the adventures of gods and heroes, ancient Greeks sought to understand the complexities of their lives and how they connected with the world around them and the deities they worshipped.

In the pages that follow, we will embark on a journey through the captivating world of Greek mythology, exploring the timeless tales of gods, heroes, and monsters that continue to enchant and inspire us today. Through these myths, we will uncover the enduring power of storytelling and the enduring relevance of ancient wisdom in our modern world.

Chapter 2

In the Beginning!

The origin stories of the Greek gods are the foundation of Greek mythology, as they explain the creation of the world and the emergence of the gods themselves.

According to Greek mythology, in the beginning, there was Chaos, a formless void from which the universe and everything within it emerged.

Gaia and Uranus were the very first creations and bore many children, including the Titans, Cyclopes, and Hecatoncheires. The Titans were the first generation of divine beings, powerful entities who ruled during the Golden Age. Among the Titans were Cronus, the youngest and most ambitious, Oceanus, Hyperion, Coeus, Crius, Iapetus, Theia, Rhea, Themis, Mnemosyne, Phoebe, and Tethys.

After some time, Uranus, fearing the power of his offspring, imprisoned the Cyclopes and the Hecatoncheires within the depths of Tartarus, a kind of Underworld. This act angered Gaia, who loved all of her children and conspired with Cronus, her youngest son, to overthrow Uranus. With Gaia's guidance, Cronus castrated Uranus, seizing power and claiming the throne as the Ruler of the Universe.

Cronus, now the king of the Titans, married his sister Rhea (yeah, I thought this was a little weird too), and they ruled over the cosmos together. However, Cronus learned of a prophecy that foretold his downfall at the hands of his own children just like his father! Fearing this prophecy, Cronus devoured each of his offspring as they were born, preventing any potential challengers to his rule.

Despite Cronus's efforts to remove his children, Rhea could not bear to see her children suffer such a fate. When she gave birth to her youngest son, Zeus, she concealed him and presented Cronus with a stone wrapped in swaddling clothes. Drunk on ambrosia, the food of immortal beings, Cronus swallowed the stone thinking that Zeus was now dealt with.

Hidden away on the island of Crete, Zeus grew up in secret, nurtured by the nymphs and protected by the divine goat Amalthea. As he matured, Zeus learned of his true heritage and his destiny to overthrow his father and free his siblings, who may have been swallowed, but not destroyed.

With help from his mother, Rhea, and his grandmother, Gaia, Zeus prepared a special drink for Cronus which made his father vomit up all of Zeus' siblings, five of them in total.

Zeus rallied his newly freed brothers and sisters to join him in a rebellion against Cronus and the Titans. The ensuing conflict, known as the Titanomachy, raged for ten years, with the Titans and their allies clashing against Zeus and his siblings.

With the aid of the Cyclopes and the Hecatoncheires, whom he freed from Tartarus, Zeus emerged victorious. He cut the immortal Cronus into pieces and cast the pieces and the Titans into the depths of Tartarus, establishing himself as the Ruler of the Universe.

Zeus and his siblings, now known as the Olympian gods and goddesses, ascended to Mount Olympus, where they established their divine court and ruled over the known universe. Each deity was assigned dominion over various aspects and places of the cosmos, from the heavens to the seas to the underworld.

Thus, the origin of the Greek gods is a tale of cosmic struggle, divine ambition, and the emergence of a new order in the universe and the struggling race of mortals that had begun to inhabit the world.

Chapter 3

The Major Gods

G reek mythology had 14 main gods, and a lot of minor gods and demi-gods or half-gods. We'll start by talking about the main gods, starting with the first six sons and daughter of Cronus and Rhea.

Zeus

God of the sky and lightning.

Sacred animal: Eagle

Zeus, the king of the gods in Greek mythology, is one of the most prominent figures in ancient Greek religion and folklore. His stories are vast and diverse, reflecting his multifaceted nature as a deity. Here are a few notable stories about Zeus:

Birth of Zeus: Zeus was the son of Cronus, the Titan ruler, and Rhea, one of the Titans. Cronus had a habit of swallowing his children to prevent them from overthrowing him, as it had been prophesied that one of his children would dethrone him. However, Rhea managed to save Zeus by tricking Cronus into swallowing a stone wrapped in swaddling clothes instead. Zeus was then secretly raised on the island of Crete by nymphs and goat herders until he reached adulthood.

Overthrow of Cronus: When Zeus reached maturity, he returned to challenge his father, Cronus, for control of the cosmos. With the help of his siblings, who would become the Olympian gods, Zeus waged a war against the Titans known as the Titanomachy. After a prolonged conflict, Zeus and his siblings emerged victorious, over-throwing Cronus and the other Titans and establishing themselves as the new ruling deities.

The Battle with the Giants (Gigantomachy): Following the Ti-tanomachy, Zeus faced another formidable challenge from the Giants, monstrous beings born from the blood of the castrated Uranus (father of Cronus). The Giants sought to overthrow the gods and rule the cosmos in their place. In response, Zeus led the Olympian gods in bat-tle against the Giants in an epic conflict known as the Gigantomachy. With the aid of the hero Heracles and other allies, Zeus eventually emerged victorious, defeating the Giants and securing the dominion of the gods.

Seductions and Affairs: Zeus was notorious for his numerous romantic liaisons and affairs with both goddesses and mortal women. He was married to Hera, the goddess of Hera, but he wandered a lot and had a lot of sons and daughters, many of whom became gods or demi-gods as well. Some of his most famous offspring include:

- Athena: Athena, the goddess of wisdom and warfare, is one of Zeus's most well-known children. She was born from Zeus's head after he swallowed her mother, Metis, to prevent a prophecy from being fulfilled. These Rulers of the Uni-verse have a real thing for swallowing people!

- Dionysus: Dionysus, the god of wine, fertility, and ecstasy, was another notable offspring of Zeus. He was born from Zeus's thigh after his mother, Semele, was consumed by

Zeus's lightning bolt.

- Heracles (Hercules): Heracles, the greatest hero of Greek mythology, was the son of Zeus and the mortal woman Alcmene. Zeus sired Heracles during one of his numerous affairs, and Heracles went on to perform many legendary feats.

Poseidon

God of the sea.

Sacred animal: Horse

Poseidon, the god of the sea, earthquakes, and horses in Greek mythology, is one of the most significant figures in ancient Greek religion and folklore. Here are a few notable stories about Poseidon:

Contest with Athena for Athens: One of the most famous stories involving Poseidon is his rivalry with the goddess Athena over the patronage of the city of Athens. According to legend, both Poseidon and Athena desired to be the city's patron deity. They agreed to a contest, each offering a gift to the people of Athens. Poseidon struck the ground with his trident, creating a spring to come up from the ground, but the water was salty and not very useful. Athena, on the other hand, presented the olive tree, which provided food, oil, and wood. The citizens of Athens chose Athena's gift, and she became the city's patroness. In his anger, Poseidon flooded parts of the city, but ultimately reconciled with Athena and became one of the city's protectors.

Creation of the Horse: Poseidon is often associated with horses, and one myth explains how he created the first horse. Poseidon was pursuing Demeter, the goddess of agriculture, who had transformed herself into a mare to escape him. Poseidon transformed himself into a stallion and captured her. From their union, the first mortal horse, Arion, was born. Poseidon later gifted the horse to the hero Adrastus.

The Creation of the Hippocampus: Poseidon is also credited with the creation of the hippocampus, a mythical creature with the upper body of a horse and the lower body of a fish. The hippocampus was often depicted as a sea creature, serving as a symbol of Poseidon's dominion over the seas.

Punishment of Odysseus: In Homer's epic poem, *the Odyssey*, Poseidon plays a significant role as the antagonist to the hero Odysseus. Poseidon harbors a grudge against Odysseus for blinding his son, the Cyclops Polyphemus, during Odysseus's journey home from the Trojan War. As a result, Poseidon continually obstructs Odysseus's journey, causing him numerous hardships and delaying his return to Ithaca.

The Creation of Islands and Landmarks: Poseidon is often depicted as the shaker of the earth, responsible for earthquakes and the creation of islands. His trident, a three-pronged spear, is said to be capable of causing earthquakes when thrust into the ground. According to myth, Poseidon often used his trident to strike the ground, creating springs, rivers, and islands.

These stories highlight Poseidon's power, influence, and complex personality as a deity associated with the sea, horses, and the natural world. He is depicted as both a benefactor and a vengeful deity, embodying the capriciousness of the ocean and the forces of nature.

Hades

God of the underworld and death.

Sacred animal: Black Ram

Hades, the god of the underworld in Greek mythology, is a figure associated with death, the afterlife, and the realm of the dead. While Hades is not as prominent in myths as some other Greek gods, there are several stories and myths in which he plays a significant role. Here are a few notable ones:

Abduction of Persephone: Perhaps the most famous story involving Hades is the abduction of Persephone, the daughter of Zeus and Demeter, the goddess of agriculture. One day, while Persephone was gathering flowers in a field, Hades emerged from the underworld and abducted her to be his wife. Demeter, grief-stricken by the loss of her daughter, searched frantically for her, causing the earth to become barren and infertile. Eventually, Zeus intervened and brokered a deal with Hades. Persephone would spend part of the year with Hades in the underworld, during which time the earth would remain barren (winter), and part of the year with her mother Demeter, during which time the earth would flourish (spring and summer).

Orpheus and Eurydice: Orpheus, a legendary musician and poet, descended into the underworld in an attempt to retrieve his wife, Eurydice, after she died from a snake bite. Hades, moved by Orpheus's music, allowed him to lead Eurydice back to the world of the living on the condition that he not look back at her until they reached the surface. However, overcome by doubt and longing, Orpheus looked back just before they emerged from the underworld, causing Eurydice to vanish back into the shadows of Hades forever.

Heracles' Twelfth Labor: As part of his Twelve Labors, Heracles (Hercules) was tasked with capturing Cerberus, the fearsome three-headed dog guarding the gates of the underworld. Heracles descended into the underworld and confronted Hades, who agreed to allow him to take Cerberus on the condition that he subdued the beast without using weapons. Heracles succeeded in overpowering

Cerberus and brought him to the surface before returning him to Hades.

Punishment of Sisyphus and Tantalus: Hades is often depicted as the judge and enforcer of punishments in the underworld. Two notable figures who received punishment in the underworld were Sisyphus and Tantalus. Sisyphus was condemned to roll a boulder up a hill for eternity, only for it to roll back down each time he reached the top. Tantalus was punished by being surrounded by food and water but unable to consume or drink anything, forever tormented by hunger and thirst.

These stories provide insight into the role of Hades as the ruler of the underworld and his interactions with mortal heroes and gods. They also illustrate themes of death, redemption, and the afterlife in Greek mythology.

Hera

Goddess of marriage and family.

Sacred animal: Cow

Hera, the queen of the gods and the wife of Zeus, is a complex figure associated with marriage, childbirth, and family. While she is often portrayed as a jealous and vengeful goddess, she is also the goddess of marriage and happy families. She plays a significant role in several myths. Here are a few notable stories involving Hera:

Birth of Hephaestus: One of the most well-known stories involving Hera is the birth of Hephaestus, the god of fire and craftsmanship. According to myth, Hera gave birth to Hephaestus without the involvement of Zeus by striking her abdomen and causing Hephaestus to emerge. Hephaestus was born deformed, and Hera, ashamed of his appearance, cast him out of Olympus. Hephaestus was later rescued by Thetis, a sea nymph, and raised in her underwater palace. Hephaestus eventually returned to Olympus and became the blacksmith of the gods.

Persecution of Heracles (Hercules): Hera harbored a deep animosity towards Heracles (Hercules), the son of Zeus and Alcmene, due to his illegitimate birth and his status as a demigod. She orchestrated numerous trials and tribulations for Heracles throughout his life, known as the "Twelve Labors of Heracles," in an attempt to thwart him. Heracles faced various challenges, including defeating the Nemean Lion, capturing the Golden Hind of Artemis, and obtaining the Golden Apples of the Hesperides, all of which were intended to be impossible tasks. Despite Hera's efforts, Heracles ultimately succeeded in completing his labors and achieving immortality.

Punishment of Zeus's Lovers: Hera frequently took vengeance on Zeus's mortal and divine lovers, as well as their offspring. One such example is Io, a mortal woman whom Zeus transformed into a heifer to conceal their affair. Hera discovered Zeus's deception and sent a gadfly to torment Io, causing her to wander the earth in anguish. Another example is Leto, the mother of Apollo and Artemis, whom Hera pursued relentlessly out of jealousy. Hera prevented Leto from giving birth on solid ground, leading to Leto's lengthy and difficult labor on the island of Delos.

The Judgement of Paris: Hera played a central role in the mythological event known as the Judgement of Paris, which ultimately led to the Trojan War. According to legend, Zeus tasked Paris, a Trojan prince, with choosing the most beautiful goddess among Hera, Athena, and Aphrodite. Each goddess offered Paris a bribe in exchange for being chosen, with Hera promising him power and authority. Ultimately, Paris chose Aphrodite as the most beautiful goddess, after she promised him the love of the most beautiful mortal woman, Helen of Sparta. Hera's resentment towards Paris and Aphrodite's role in his decision led to the Trojan War.

These stories highlight Hera's complex personality and her role as both a powerful goddess and a vindictive figure in Greek mythology. She is depicted as a protector of marriage and family, but also as a formidable adversary to those who cross her or defy her authority.

Demeter

Goddess of agriculture and wheat.

Sacred animal: Serpent

Demeter, the goddess of agriculture, fertility, and the harvest in Greek mythology, is a central figure in many myths, particularly those concerning the cycle of the seasons and the growth of crops. Here are a few notable stories involving Demeter:

Abduction of Persephone: Perhaps the most famous myth involving Demeter is the abduction of her daughter Persephone by Hades, the god of the underworld. According to the myth, while Persephone was gathering flowers in a meadow, Hades emerged from the earth and abducted her to be his wife. Demeter, grief-stricken by the loss of her daughter, searched tirelessly for her, neglecting her duties as the goddess of agriculture. As a result, the earth became barren and infertile, which wasn't good for the mortals trying to live there. Eventually, Zeus intervened and brokered a deal with Hades. Persephone would spend part of the year with Hades in the underworld, during which time the earth would remain barren (winter), and part of the year with her mother Demeter, during which time the earth would flourish (spring and summer).

Demeter and Triptolemus: After the abduction of Persephone, Demeter wandered the earth in search of her daughter. In her grief, she came to the palace of King Celeus of Eleusis, disguised as an old woman. The king and queen welcomed Demeter into their home and asked her to nurse their son, Demophon. To show her gratitude, Demeter decided to bestow immortality upon the child. Each night, she placed Demophon in the fire to burn away his mortality, but the queen, horrified by the sight, interrupted the ritual. In response, Demeter revealed her true identity and instructed the king to build a temple in her honor. She also taught Triptolemus, the king's other son, the secrets of agriculture and sent him out into the world to teach humanity how to cultivate crops.

Demeter and the Eleusinian Mysteries: The Eleusinian Mysteries were secret religious rites and ceremonies dedicated to Demeter and Persephone, celebrated in the town of Eleusis in ancient Greece. The exact nature of the mysteries remains shrouded in secrecy, as participants were sworn to secrecy under penalty of death. However, it is believed that the rituals involved the celebration of the cycle of life, death, and rebirth, symbolized by the story of Demeter and Persephone.

The Homeric Hymn to Demeter: The Homeric Hymn to Demeter is an ancient Greek poem that tells the story of Demeter's search for Persephone and her grief over her daughter's abduction. The hymn provides insight into the rituals and beliefs surrounding the Eleusinian Mysteries and emphasizes the importance of agriculture and fertility in ancient Greek society.

These stories highlight Demeter's role as a nurturing mother goddess and her association with the fertility of the earth and the cycle of the seasons. She is revered as a fierce mother as shown by her search for her lost daughter, a protector of agriculture and the harvest, as well as a symbol of renewal and growth.

Hestia

Goddess of the hearth and home.

Sacred animal: Pig

Hestia, the Greek goddess of the hearth, home, and family, is a less prominent figure in Greek mythology compared to some of the other Olympian gods and goddesses. However, she is still revered as a symbol of domesticity, hospitality, and the sacred flame of the hearth. Here are a few stories and aspects of Hestia's mythology:

The First and Last: Hestia is often referred to as the first and last of the Olympian gods. This designation signifies her importance as the eldest daughter of Cronus and Rhea, making her the first to be swallowed by Cronus and the last to be regurgitated by him during his conflict with Zeus. As a result, Hestia is sometimes depicted as a symbol of continuity and stability within the divine order.

The Hearth and Home: Hestia's primary role in Greek mythology is as the goddess of the hearth, representing the sacred fire that burned in the center of the home. The hearth has long been considered the focal point of domestic life, where families gather for meals and offerings are made to the gods. Hestia's presence symbolized warmth, security, and hospitality, and she was invoked at the beginning and end of important events, such as meals and sacrifices.

Vesta in Roman Mythology: In Roman mythology, Hestia is identified with the goddess Vesta, who also presided over the hearth and home. The Vestal Virgins, priestesses dedicated to Vesta, tended the sacred fire in her temple in Rome, ensuring its perpetual burning. Like Hestia, Vesta was honored as a guardian of the family and community, and her worship played a central role in Roman religious rituals.

A Quiet Presence: Unlike some of the other Olympian gods and goddesses, Hestia does not feature prominently in many myths or legends. She is often depicted as a gentle and peaceful deity, preferring solitude and contemplation to the drama and conflicts that frequently ensnared her divine relatives. Hestia's quiet presence serves as a reminder of the importance of simplicity, harmony, and inner tranquility in both the divine and mortal realms.

While Hestia may not have as many stories associated with her as some of the other Olympian gods and goddesses, her role as the goddess of the hearth and home was essential in ancient Greek culture, symbolizing the warmth, stability, and unity of the family and community.

These six gods are the original children of Cronus and Rhea, but there were others who were born to gods or rose to those positions as part of the 14-member pantheon.

Athena

Goddess of defense and wisdom.

Sacred animal: Owl

Athena, the Greek goddess of wisdom, warfare, and crafts, is one of the most prominent and revered figures in Greek mythology. Known for her intelligence, strategic prowess, and sense of justice, Athena is associated with various myths and stories. Here are some notable ones:

Birth of Athena: According to myth, Athena was born fully grown and wearing armor from the forehead of her father, Zeus. This unusual birth occurred after Zeus swallowed Metis, the goddess of wisdom and craft, who was pregnant with Athena. Hephaestus, the god of fire and craftsmanship, split Zeus's skull with an axe, allowing Athena to emerge.

The Contest with Poseidon: Athena and Poseidon, the god of the sea, competed for patronage of the city of Athens. Each deity offered a gift to the people of Athens, and the citizens were to choose which gift they preferred. Poseidon struck the ground with his trident, creating a saltwater spring, while Athena planted the first olive tree. The citizens chose Athena's gift, as the olive tree provided food, oil, and wood, signifying peace and prosperity.

The Judgment of Paris: Athena was one of the three goddesses (along with Hera and Aphrodite) who vied for the golden apple inscribed with "to the fairest" thrown by Eris, the goddess of discord, at the wedding of Peleus and Thetis. Zeus tasked Paris, a Trojan prince, with judging which goddess was the fairest. Each goddess offered Paris a bribe, with Athena promising him wisdom and victory in battle. Paris ultimately chose Aphrodite as the most beautiful, leading to the events that sparked the Trojan War.

The Contest with Arachne: Arachne, a mortal weaver, boasted that her skills at the loom surpassed those of Athena herself. Offended by Arachne's arrogance, Athena challenged her to a weaving contest. Both Arachne and Athena created exquisite tapestries, but Athena's depicted the gods in a more favorable light, while Arachne's mocked them. In her anger, Athena transformed Arachne into a spider, condemning her to weave webs for eternity.

Athena and Heracles (Hercules): Athena aided Heracles (Hercules) in various tasks and quests throughout his life. She provided him with wisdom, guidance, and divine assistance, particularly during his Twelve Labors. Athena also played a role in Heracles's apotheosis, assisting him in his ascension to Mount Olympus after his death.

These stories highlight Athena's multifaceted character as a goddess of wisdom, strategy, and justice, as well as her influence in both divine and mortal affairs. She is revered as a patron of heroes, artisans, and cities, embodying the ideals of intelligence, courage, and civilization in Greek mythology.

Ares

God of war.

Sacred animal: Wild Boar

Ares, the Greek god of war, is a complex figure in Greek mythology, often depicted as a violent and bloodthirsty deity who relishes conflict and battle. Here are some notable stories and aspects of Ares's mythology:

Parentage and Characterization: Ares is the son of Zeus, the king of the gods, and Hera, the queen of the gods. He is often portrayed as a hot-headed and impulsive god, driven by his love for battle and conquest. Despite his association with the valor of war, Ares is not always depicted in a favorable light in Greek mythology, as he is portrayed as cowardly and easily wounded as often as he is fierce and victorious.

Affairs and Relationships: Ares is known for his romantic liaisons and relationships with various goddesses and mortal women. One of his most famous affairs was with Aphrodite, the goddess of love and beauty, which resulted in a scandalous love triangle involving Aphrodite's husband, Hephaestus, the god of fire and craftsmanship. Ares and Aphrodite were often depicted together, symbolizing the passionate and destructive aspects of love and desire.

The Trojan War: Ares played a significant role in the Trojan War, siding with the Trojans against the Greeks. He was a fierce and formidable warrior, inspiring fear and terror on the battlefield. Ares intervened in battles to aid the Trojans, often clashing with Athena, the goddess of wisdom and strategic warfare, who supported the Greek forces. Ares's involvement in the war contributed to its bloody and destructive nature.

The Loves of Ares: In addition to his affair with Aphrodite, Ares had other romantic entanglements and offspring. He fathered several children with various goddesses and mortal women, including Phobos (Fear), Deimos (Terror), and Eros (Desire). These offspring embodied the aspects of war and violence associated with their father, contributing to the chaos and conflict of the mortal world.

Punishment and Humiliation: Despite his prowess in battle, Ares was not invincible, and he suffered humiliation and defeat on several occasions. In one myth, Ares was captured and imprisoned by the Aloadae, twin giants who sought to overthrow the gods. In another myth, Ares was wounded and driven from the battlefield by the mortal hero Diomedes during the Trojan War, highlighting his vulnerability and mortality.

These stories illustrate the complex and often contradictory nature of Ares as the god of war in Greek mythology. While he embodies the violence and chaos of battle, he is also subject to humiliation and defeat, highlighting the fickle and unpredictable nature of war itself.

Hephaestus

God of fire and craftsmen.

Sacred animal: Donkey

Hephaestus, the Greek god of fire, blacksmiths, craftsmen, and volcanoes, is a fascinating figure in Greek mythology. Here are some notable stories and aspects of Hephaestus's mythology:

Birth of Hephaestus: Hephaestus was born to Zeus, the king of the gods, and Hera, his wife and queen. However, Hera gave birth to Hephaestus without the involvement of Zeus, either as an act of defiance or as a response to Zeus's own birth of Athena. In some versions of the myth, Hephaestus is born deformed or lame, which leads Hera to reject him and cast him out of Olympus, but he always is restored to his position despite his rough beginnings.

Hephaestus and the Forge: Hephaestus was known as a skilled blacksmith and craftsman, and he was often depicted working at his forge, crafting intricate weapons, armor, and other artifacts for the gods and heroes. His forge was located beneath the volcanic Mount Etna in Sicily, where he crafted his creations with the help of his assistants, the Cyclopes.

Marriage to Aphrodite: Despite his deformity, Hephaestus became enamored with Aphrodite, the goddess of love and beauty and they were eventually married. However, Aphrodite was involved with to the god of war, Ares. In some versions of the myth, Hephaestus used his ingenuity to ensnare Aphrodite and Ares in a golden net while they were together, exposing their affair to the other gods.

Creation of Pandora: Hephaestus played a role in the creation of Pandora, the first woman in Greek mythology. According to the myth, Hephaestus crafted Pandora out of clay at the command of Zeus, who intended her to be a punishment for humanity. Pandora was endowed with various gifts from the gods, including curiosity, and she unwittingly released all manner of evils into the world when she opened a jar (often mistakenly referred to as a box) given to her by Zeus.

Hephaestus and the Aeneid: In Virgil's epic poem, the Aeneid, Hephaestus is depicted as assisting Aeneas, the legendary founder of Rome, in his various quests. Hephaestus forges new armor and weapons for Aeneas, including a shield decorated with scenes of Roman history and prophecy. The shield plays a crucial role in Aeneas's journey and eventual victory.

Hephaestus's Return to Olympus: Despite being rejected by Hera and encountering various challenges, Hephaestus eventually returns to Olympus and is reconciled with the other gods. He becomes renowned for his craftsmanship and ingenuity, creating magnificent works of art and technology for both the gods and mortal heroes. His deformity is seen as a sign that even someone at an extreme disadvantage can be clever and worthwhile.

These stories highlight Hephaestus's role as a skilled craftsman and inventor, as well as his complex relationships with the other gods and his enduring contributions to Greek mythology.

Aphrodite

Goddess of beauty.

Sacred animal: Dove

Aphrodite, the Greek goddess of love, beauty, desire, and fertility, is a central figure in Greek mythology. She is often the source of conflict as both gods and mortals try to impress her and win the love she promises. Here are some notable stories and aspects of Aphrodite's mythology:

Birth of Aphrodite: Aphrodite's origins vary depending on the mythological tradition. In one version of the myth, Aphrodite is born from the sea foam that forms around the severed genitals of Uranus, the primordial sky god, which were thrown into the sea by his son, Cronus. In another version, Aphrodite is the daughter of Zeus, the king of the gods, and Dione, a Titaness. Regardless of her origins, Aphrodite is associated with the sea and is often depicted emerging from the waves.

Marriage to Hephaestus: Aphrodite is married to Hephaestus, the god of fire and blacksmiths, in an arranged marriage by Zeus.

However, Aphrodite is not faithful to Hephaestus and has numerous affairs, most notably with Ares, the god of war. Hephaestus is aware of Aphrodite's infidelity and even catches her in the act with Ares, but despite all of his efforts he is unable to win her affections.

Judgment of Paris: One of the most famous stories involving Aphrodite is the Judgment of Paris, which ultimately leads to the Trojan War. Eris, the goddess of discord, throws a golden apple inscribed with the words "to the fairest" among the goddesses Hera, Athena, and Aphrodite at the wedding of Peleus and Thetis. Each goddess claims the apple for herself, leading Zeus to task Paris, a Trojan prince, with judging which goddess is the fairest. Each goddess offers Paris a bribe, and Aphrodite promises him the love of the most beautiful mortal woman, Helen of Sparta. Paris chooses Aphrodite as the winner, leading to his abduction of Helen and the subsequent Trojan War.

Affairs and Offspring: Aphrodite is associated with numerous love affairs and offspring in Greek mythology. She is the mother of Eros, the god of love, who assists her in her romantic exploits. Aphrodite is also the mother of numerous mortal and divine children, including Harmonia, the goddess of harmony, and Aeneas, the legendary founder of Rome. These offspring embody the passions and desires associated with Aphrodite's domain.

Cult and Worship: Aphrodite was worshipped throughout the ancient Greek world, particularly in the city of Corinth, where she had a famous temple dedicated to her. She was often invoked by individuals seeking love, fertility, and beauty, and her cult rituals included festivals, sacrifices, and offerings.

These stories highlight Aphrodite's role as the embodiment of love, desire, and beauty in Greek mythology, as well as her influence in both divine and mortal affairs. She is revered as a powerful and influential goddess, capable of inspiring passion and desire in both gods and mortals alike.

Apollo

God of medicine and music.

Sacred animal: Sun Cow

Apollo, the Greek god of light, prophecy, healing, music, poetry, and more, is one of the most significant and multifaceted figures in Greek mythology. Here are some notable stories and aspects of Apollo's mythology:

Birth of Apollo: Apollo was born on the island of Delos to Zeus, the king of the gods, and Leto, a Titaness. His birth was significant because Leto had been pursued by the jealous Hera, who had cursed her to be unable to give birth on any land touched by the sun. Delos, being a floating island, was not considered land, allowing Leto to safely give birth to Apollo and his twin sister, Artemis, the goddess of the hunt.

Apollo and the Python: In his infancy, Apollo killed the serpent Python, a monstrous creature born from the mud and slime left behind after the great flood of Deucalion. Python had been terrorizing the region of Delphi, and Apollo slew the creature with his bow and arrows. Afterward, Apollo claimed Delphi as his sacred site and established the famous Oracle at Delphi, where he dispensed prophecies to mortals.

Apollo and Daphne: In one of the most famous myths involving Apollo, the god fell in love with the nymph Daphne. However, Daphne rejected Apollo's advances and fled from him. Apollo pursued Daphne relentlessly, but as he closed in on her, she prayed to her father, a river god, to save her. Her father transformed her into a laurel tree, and Apollo, unable to possess her, declared the laurel tree sacred to him and vowed to wear its leaves as a crown.

Apollo and the Music Contest: Apollo was a skilled musician and played the lyre, an instrument he received from Hermes, the messenger god. In a musical contest with the satyr Marsyas, Apollo played his lyre, while Marsyas played the flute. Despite Marsyas's impressive performance, Apollo emerged victorious. Despite winning, Apollo flayed Marsyas alive as punishment for his hubris.

Apollo and the Trojan War: Apollo played a significant role in the events of the Trojan War. He supported the Trojans and intervened in battles on their behalf, often clashing with the Greek hero Achilles. Apollo aided Paris in shooting his arrow that fatally wounded Achilles in his heel, the only vulnerable spot on his body. Apollo's involvement in the war contributed to the fall of Troy.

Apollo's Healing and Prophecy: Apollo was also revered as a healer and the god of prophecy. His sanctuary at Delphi served as a renowned center for prophecy and healing, where pilgrims sought guidance and cures for their ailments. Apollo's priests, known as the Pythia, delivered his prophecies to seekers who consulted the oracle.

These stories highlight Apollo's diverse attributes and roles as a god of the sun, music, healing, prophecy, and more. He is revered as a patron of the arts, a source of inspiration and wisdom, and a powerful force in both the mortal and divine realms.

Artemis

Goddess of children, and hunting.

Sacred animal: Dog/Wolf

Birth of Artemis: Artemis was born on the island of Delos to Zeus, the king of the gods, and Leto, a Titaness. Her birth was significant because Leto had been pursued by the jealous Hera, who had cursed her to be unable to give birth on any land touched by the sun. Delos, being a floating island, was not considered land, allowing Leto to safely give birth to Artemis and her twin brother, Apollo.

Artemis and Actaeon: In one of the most famous myths involving Artemis, the hunter Actaeon stumbled upon her while she was bathing in a sacred spring. Furious at being seen naked, Artemis transformed Actaeon into a stag, and he was subsequently torn apart by his own hunting dogs. This myth highlights Artemis's fierce and uncompromising nature, as well as her role as a protector of her sacred spaces.

Artemis and Orion: Artemis was also associated with the myth of Orion, a skilled hunter and her hunting companion. Different versions of the myth exist, but one common story tells of Orion's death at the hands of a giant scorpion sent by Gaia, the earth goddess. Distraught over Orion's death, Artemis placed him among the stars as the constellation Orion.

Artemis and Niobe: Another famous myth involving Artemis is the story of Niobe, a queen who boasted of her many children, surpassing those of Leto. Offended by Niobe's arrogance, Artemis and Apollo, her twin brother, sought revenge. They killed all of Niobe's children, leaving her grief-stricken. Niobe's story serves as a cautionary tale against hubris and arrogance.

Artemis and the Amazons: Artemis was also associated with the Amazons, a tribe of warrior women. She was sometimes depicted as their patron goddess, aiding them in battle and guiding them in their pursuits. Artemis's association with the Amazons underscores her role as a protector of women and a symbol of female strength and independence.

Artemis and the Wild Animals: As the goddess of the hunt and wilderness, Artemis was often depicted in stories and art with wild animals such as deer, bears, and hounds. She was revered as a skilled archer and hunter, roaming the forests and mountains with her companions and protecting the natural world and its inhabitants.

These stories highlight Artemis's diverse attributes and roles as a goddess of the hunt, wilderness, childbirth, and virginity. She is revered as a fierce and independent deity, embodying the untamed spirit of the natural world and serving as a symbol of strength, purity, and protection.

Hermes

God of cattle herding, thieves, travelers, roads.

Sacred animal: Tortoise

Hermes, the Greek god of commerce, communication, travelers, thieves, and messenger of the gods, is a fascinating figure in Greek mythology. Here are some notable stories and aspects of Hermes's mythology:

Birth of Hermes: Hermes is the son of Zeus, the king of the gods, and Maia, a nymph and one of the Pleiades. He was born in a cave on Mount Cyllene in Arcadia, and from his infancy, he displayed cunning, cleverness, and a mischievous nature.

The Theft of Apollo's Cattle: One of the most famous myths involving Hermes is the story of his theft of Apollo's cattle shortly after his birth. Hermes fashioned a lyre from a tortoise shell and used it to play music while tending to Apollo's cattle. They loved the music and when he walked away, the cows followed him! When Apollo discovered that his cattle were missing, he accused Hermes of theft. Zeus intervened and mediated between the two gods, and Hermes returned Apollo's cattle in exchange for Apollo's golden staff, known as the caduceus, which became one of Hermes's symbols.

Messenger of the Gods: Hermes is best known for his role as the messenger of the gods, tasked with delivering messages between the gods and mortals. He is often depicted wearing winged sandals and a winged hat, symbols of his speed and agility. Hermes also guided the souls of the dead to the underworld as a psychopomp, ensuring safe passage to the afterlife.

Invention of the Pan Pipes: According to myth, Hermes invented the pan pipes, also known as the syrinx, after falling in love with the nymph Syrinx. Syrinx, wishing to escape Hermes's advances, transformed herself into a clump of reeds. Hermes, saddened by her disappearance, fashioned the pan pipes from the reeds and used them to create music in her memory.

Association with Thieves and Trickery: Hermes was also associated with thieves, trickery, and deception. He was worshipped by thieves and rogues who sought his protection and guidance in their illicit activities. Hermes was revered as a cunning and resourceful deity who outwitted his adversaries through cleverness and ingenuity over strength.

Hermes in the Argonautica: In the epic poem *Argonautica* by Apollonius of Rhodes, Hermes aids the hero Jason and the Argonauts in their quest for the Golden Fleece. He provides guidance and assistance to Jason throughout his journey, ensuring the success of the Argonauts in their perilous quest.

These stories highlight Hermes's diverse attributes and roles as a god of communication, commerce, travelers, and trickery. He is revered as a clever and resourceful deity, capable of navigating the complexities of both the divine and mortal worlds.

Dionysus

God of wine and parties.

Sacred animal: Panther

Dionysus, the Greek god of wine, fertility, ecstasy, and theater, is a complex and influential figure in Greek mythology. Here are some notable stories and aspects of Dionysus's mythology:

Birth of Dionysus: Dionysus's birth is one of the most famous stories in Greek mythology. He was born to Zeus, the king of the gods, and Semele, a mortal woman and daughter of Cadmus, the king of Thebes. Hera, Zeus's jealous wife, tricked Semele into asking Zeus to reveal himself in his full divine glory, which resulted in her being consumed by Zeus's lightning bolts. Zeus rescued the unborn Dionysus and sewed him into his thigh until he was ready to be born. Dionysus's unusual birth and divine parentage are central to his mythological significance.

Journey of Dionysus: Dionysus is often depicted as a wanderer, traveling throughout the world to spread his worship and teachings. He encountered various challenges and adventures during his journeys, including encounters with pirates, giants, and hostile kings. These myths emphasize Dionysus's status as a god of ecstasy, liberation, and transformation, as well as his association with revelry and madness.

Dionysus and the Bacchae: One of the most well known myths involving Dionysus is the story of his return to Thebes, his birthplace, where he sought to establish his worship. Despite resistance from King Pentheus, who opposed Dionysus's worship, Dionysus inspired the women of Thebes, known as the Bacchae, to join his ecstatic rites and revelries. In a fit of madness, Pentheus disguised himself as a woman and spied on the Bacchae, but he was ultimately torn apart by them in a frenzied Dionysian ritual.

The Maenads and Satyrs: Dionysus's followers, known as Maenads and Satyrs, were known for their wild and uninhibited behavior. The Maenads, female devotees of Dionysus, would participate in ecstatic rituals and dances, often accompanied by music and wine. Satyrs, male companions of Dionysus, were half-man, half-goat creatures known for their lustful and mischievous nature. Together, they embodied the Dionysian spirit of revelry and abandon.

Dionysus in Drama: Dionysus was closely associated with the development of theater in ancient Greece. The Dionysia, festivals held in honor of Dionysus, featured dramatic performances of tragedies, comedies, and satyr plays. Dionysus was revered as the patron god of theater and inspiration for playwrights, actors, and artists.

Dionysus and Ariadne: Dionysus fell in love with Ariadne, the daughter of King Minos of Crete, after she was abandoned by Theseus on the island of Naxos. Dionysus married Ariadne and later placed her crown, the Corona Borealis, in the sky as a constellation.

These stories highlight Dionysus's diverse attributes and roles as a god of wine, ecstasy, theater, and fertility. He is revered as a liberator, bringing joy, madness, and transformation to those who follow him, while also embodying the dualities of civilization and wildness, order and chaos.

You would think that 14 gods would be plenty to write stories about, but we're only getting started! Next we'll talk about some of the prominent heroes of Ancient Greece!

Chapter 4

The Heroes

While the stories of the Gods were some of the most retold, just as important to the ancient greeks were the stories of Heroes. These were brave men and women (often half-gods themselves) who were given great tasks and accomplished great deeds, but rarely without a price. There were always things to learn in the stories of the heroes from bravery and sacrifice, to the price of hubris and defying the gods! Here are some of the most famous heroes and their deeds:

Hercules

Hercules, also known as Heracles in Greek mythology, is one of the most famous and celebrated heroes of ancient Greece. His story is filled with epic feats, incredible strength, and numerous adventures. Here's an overview of the story of Hercules:

Birth and Childhood: Hercules was the son of Zeus, the king of the gods, and Alcmene, a mortal woman. Zeus conceived Hercules while disguised as Alcmene's husband, Amphitryon. Hera, Zeus's wife and Hercules's stepmother, held a grudge against Hercules due to his illegitimate birth and sought to destroy him from the moment of his conception. It might have been more fair for them to be mad at Zeus, but their anger did drive Hercules to become an amazing hero.

The Twelve Labors: Hercules is most renowned for his Twelve Labors, a series of tasks given to him by King Eurystheus of Tiryns as a form of penance for killing his own wife and children in a fit of madness induced by Hera. The labors are as follows:

- ***Slay the Nemean Lion***: Hercules strangled the invulnerable lion with his bare hands.

- ***Slay the Hydra of Lerna:*** Hercules defeated the multi-headed serpent by cutting off its heads, while his nephew Iolaus cauterized the necks to prevent them from regrowing.

- ***Capture the Golden Hind of Artemis:*** Hercules captured the sacred deer alive.

- ***Capture the Erymanthian Boar:*** Hercules subdued the massive boar on Mount Erymanthus.

- ***Clean the Augean Stables:*** Hercules diverted the course of two rivers to cleanse the filthy stables of King Augeas in a single day.

- ***Slay the Stymphalian Birds:*** Hercules drove away the man-eating birds that plagued Lake Stymphalis with the help of Athena.

- ***Capture the Cretan Bull:*** Hercules captured the rampaging bull sent by Poseidon.

- ***Steal the Mares of Diomedes:*** Hercules stole the man-eating horses of Diomedes, the Thracian king, and fed Diomedes to them.

- ***Obtain the belt of Hippolyta:*** Hercules retrieved the magical belt of the Amazon queen Hippolyta.

- ***Steal the Cattle of Geryon:*** Hercules stole the cattle of Geryon, a giant with three bodies, from the far western edge of the world.

- ***Steal the Apples of the Hesperides:*** Hercules retrieved the golden apples from the garden of the Hesperides, aided by Atlas.

- ***Capture Cerberus, the Hound of Hades:*** Hercules journeyed to the underworld and captured Cerberus, the fearsome three-headed dog that guards the gates of Hades.

Other Adventures: Apart from the Twelve Labors, Hercules undertook numerous other adventures, including his involvement in the Argonauts' quest for the Golden Fleece, his battle with the centaurs, and his wrestling match with Antaeus, among others.

Tragic Events: Despite his heroic deeds, Hercules faced several tragic events in his life, including being driven mad by Hera and killing his wife and children. As penance, he willingly accepted the Twelve Labors.

Death and Deification: Hercules eventually met his end through a combination of factors. He was poisoned by the centaur Nessus, but before succumbing to the poison, he built his own funeral pyre. He ascended the pyre and was consumed by the flames, achieving immortality and joining the gods on Mount Olympus.

Hercules's story is one of valor, strength, and the struggle against fate. His exploits have inspired countless works of art, literature, and cinema, making him one of the most enduring figures of Greek mythology.

Theseus

Theseus was a legendary hero and the son of King Aegeus of Athens, although his parentage is sometimes attributed to the god Poseidon as well. His adventures are numerous and varied, with some of the most well-known being:

Birth and Childhood: Theseus was born in Troezen, a city in the northeastern Peloponnese. His mother, Aethra, had relations with both Aegeus and Poseidon on the same night, resulting in Theseus being born with two potential fathers. When he came of age, Aethra revealed his true parentage and directed him to find his father in Athens.

The Journey to Athens: Theseus embarked on a journey to Athens, facing various challenges along the way. Most notably, he encountered and defeated a number of villains and monsters, including Periphetes (the Club Bearer), Sinis (the Pine Bender), Sciron (the Scammer), and Procrustes (the Stretcher), all of whom he dispatched in gruesome fashion, using their own methods against them.

Arrival in Athens and the Minotaur: Upon reaching Athens, Theseus faced the challenge of the Minotaur, a monstrous creature with the body of a man and the head of a bull. The Minotaur was kept in the labyrinth constructed by King Minos of Crete. Every year, Athens was forced to send seven young men and seven maidens as tribute to be devoured by the Minotaur. Theseus volunteered to be one of the sacrificial victims and, with the help of Princess Ariadne, daughter of King Minos, he successfully navigated the labyrinth and slew the Minotaur.

Return to Athens and the Death of Aegeus: When he returned to Athens, Theseus forgot to change the color of his sails from black to white, a signal to his father Aegeus that he was returning victorious from Crete. Seeing the black sails, Aegeus, thinking his son was dead, threw himself into the sea, which was then named the Aegean Sea in his honor. Theseus thus became king of Athens.

Adventures as King: Theseus performed various deeds as king, including the establishment of the Isthmian Games in honor of Poseidon, and the unification of Attica (the region surrounding Athens). He also participated in the Calydonian Boar Hunt and the quest for the Golden Fleece.

Later Years and Death: In his later years, Theseus faced challenges to his rule, including a war with the Amazons led by Queen Hippolyta. He married several times, with his most famous wife being Phaedra. In the end, he fell from favor and was banished from Athens. He sought refuge in the island of Skyros, where he was either murdered or pushed off a cliff by the local king, Lycomedes.

The story of Theseus is rich with heroism, adventure, and the overcoming of formidable challenges, making him one of the most celebrated heroes in Greek mythology.

Perseus

Perseus is another famous hero from Greek mythology. His tale is filled with adventure, heroism, and divine intervention. Here's an overview of Perseus's story:

Birth and Prophecy: Perseus was the son of Zeus, the king of the gods, and Danaë, a mortal princess. A prophecy foretold that Danaë's son would one day kill her father, Acrisius, the king of Argos. Fearing the prophecy, Acrisius locked Danaë and Perseus in a chest and cast them into the sea. The chest washed ashore on the island of Seriphos and they emerged, unhurt, but probably hungry.

Perseus and Polydectes: On Seriphos, Perseus and Danaë were taken in by Dictys, a fisherman, and his family. However, Polydectes, the tyrant ruler of Seriphos, became infatuated with Danaë and sought to marry her. To rid himself of Perseus, Polydectes sent him on a seemingly impossible quest: to bring him the head of the Gorgon, Medusa.

The Quest for Medusa's Head: Perseus, aided by divine gifts from the gods, set out on his quest to slay the Gorgon. He received a reflective shield from Athena, winged sandals from Hermes, and a sword from Hephaestus. Perseus also obtained guidance from the Graeae, three old women who shared one eye and one tooth between them.

Encounter with Medusa: Perseus journeyed to the far-off land of the Gorgons, where he found Medusa and her sisters sleeping. With the help of Athena's shield which he used to avoid direct eye contact and using his polished shield as a mirror, Perseus managed to decapitate Medusa while she slept, taking care not to look directly at her. From her severed neck sprang forth the winged horse Pegasus and the giant Chrysaor. In some myths, Pegasus became Perseus' mount, while others assign the winged horse to Hercules.

Rescue of Andromeda: On his journey back home, Perseus encountered Andromeda, a princess who was chained to a rock as a sacrifice to a sea monster. He fell in love with her at first sight. Perseus slayed the monster, saving Andromeda, and later married her.

Confrontation with Acrisius: Perseus returned to Seriphos to find that Polydectes had mistreated his mother. In a fit of rage, Perseus used Medusa's head to turn Polydectes and his followers into stone.

Perseus then revealed his identity to Dictys and made him king of Seriphos.

Fulfillment of the Prophecy: Perseus participated in athletic games held in honor of King Acrisius. During a discus-throwing contest, Perseus accidentally struck Acrisius, fulfilling the prophecy of causing his grandfather's death.

Legacy: Perseus and Andromeda had several children, including Perses, who would become the ancestor of the Persians. Perseus also became the founder of the city of Mycenae.

The story of Perseus is a classic tale of heroism, adventure, and destiny, showcasing the importance of courage, resourcefulness, and divine favor in overcoming seemingly insurmountable obstacles.

Bellerophone

The story of **Bellerophon**, also spelled as Bellerophontes, is another fascinating tale from Greek mythology, though it may not be as widely known as those of Hercules, Theseus, or Perseus. Here's an overview of Bellerophon's story:

Birth and Early Life: Bellerophon was the son of Glaucus, the king of Corinth, and the grandson of Sisyphus. His lineage was noble, but his fate was marked by both triumph and tragedy. Bellerophon's early life was unremarkable until he was accused of killing a man while practicing his knife throwing with his friends, resulting in his exile from Corinth.

Exiled: During his exile, Bellerophon sought refuge in the court of King Proetus of Tiryns. Queen Anteia, wife of Proetus, fell in love with Bellerophon but was spurned. In revenge, she falsely accused Bellerophon of attempting to seduce her. King Proetus, unwilling to kill a guest, sent Bellerophon to his father-in-law, King Iobates of

Lycia, with a sealed letter requesting his death. However, Iobates, also hesitant to kill a guest, devised a series of seemingly impossible tasks for Bellerophon, hoping that he would perish attempting them.

The Slaying of the Chimera: One of the tasks assigned to Bellerophon was to kill the Chimera, a fearsome creature with the body of a lion, the head of a goat, and the tail of a serpent, who was capable of breathing fire. On his way to find the Chimera, Bellerophon was given a prophecy that he would need help from the winged horse, Pegasus. He was aided by the goddess Athena, who loaned him a magical bridle, and managed to tame the winged horse Pegasus, who was born from the blood of the Gorgon Medusa when Perseus beheaded her. Riding Pegasus, Bellerophon flew above the Chimera and rained down arrows on it, ultimately defeating the beast.

Other Exploits: Emboldened by his success, Bellerophon undertook further adventures. He fought and defeated the Amazons, a tribe of warrior women, and the Solymi, a fierce mountain tribe. He also battled the Lycian forces alongside their king, Iobates, earning his gratitude and forgiveness for the false accusations.

Hubris and Downfall: Despite his heroic deeds, Bellerophon's story takes a tragic turn. Filled with pride and arrogance, he attempted to fly Pegasus to the summit of Mount Olympus, the realm of the gods, hoping to join them. Zeus, angered by this hubris, sent a gadfly to sting Pegasus, causing Bellerophon to fall to the earth below. Bellerophon survived the fall but was left crippled and blinded, wandering in misery for the rest of his days.

Legacy: Despite his downfall, Bellerophon is remembered as a hero of Greek mythology, particularly for his slaying of the Chimera. Pegasus, the winged horse, continued to be revered and became a symbol of inspiration and divine aid.

The story of Bellerophon serves as a cautionary tale about the dangers of pride and arrogance, as well as the consequences of defying the will of the gods.

Famous Stories

Not all of the most famous myths were about heroes, though they all included people who were heroic in their own way. Let's talk about some of the other famous people and stories from Greek Mythology, starting with Daedalus and Icarus.

Daedalus

Daedalus is a unique type of hero in Greek Mythology as his deeds weren't feats of strength or valor, but of cunning and skill. The most well known story he is associate with concerns the building of the minotaur's labyrinth and his escape from King Minos after the labyrinth was completed. The story goes something like this:

Daedalus was born into a family of skilled craftsmen and artists in the kingdom of Athens. His father was a renowned inventor and architect, and from a young age, Daedalus showed a similar aptitude for creativity and innovation. He spent his childhood exploring the workshops and studios of his family, learning the intricacies of craftsmanship and design. As he grew older, Daedalus developed his own unique style, gaining a reputation as one of the most talented artisans in Athens.

Daedalus' talents caught the attention of King Minos of Crete, who sought his services to build the Labyrinth, a vast and intricate maze intended to contain the Minotaur, a monstrous creature with the body of a man and the head of a bull. Daedalus accepted the commission, however, as work on the Labyrinth progressed, tensions between Daedalus and King Minos grew. The king's demands became unreasonable, and Daedalus found himself caught in a web of political intrigue and personal rivalries. When the warrior Theseus arrived, Daedalus told the secret of the Labyrinth to the king's daughter who used it to help save the man she had fallen in love with.

Angered by Daedalus' actions, King Minos ordered the craftsman and his son, Icarus, to be imprisoned within the very maze they had constructed. Trapped within the labyrinth's twisting corridors and hidden passages, Daedalus faced the daunting challenge of finding a way to escape. Determined to regain his freedom and ensure the safety of his son, Daedalus devised a daring plan that would test all of his skills.

Drawing inspiration from the flight of birds and the delicate mechanics of nature, he decided to create wings that would allow him and Icarus to soar above the maze and reach the safety of the outside world. Gathering feathers from birds and wax harvested from bees, Daedalus fashioned the wings with meticulous care and precision. Each feather was carefully attached to a framework of wax, forming the shape of wings.

With the wings completed, Daedalus and Icarus prepared to make their daring escape. Daedalus instructed his son on the proper use of the wings, cautioning him against flying too close to the sun, whose heat would melt the wax, or too close to the sea, whose moisture would dampen the feathers. As they launched themselves into the air, the exhilarating sensation of flight filled them with a sense of freedom. For a brief moment, they soared together, father and son, bound by a shared dream of escape and redemption.

But as they ascended higher and higher into the sky, Icarus became intoxicated by the thrill of flight, heedless of his father's warnings.

Ignoring Daedalus' advice, he flew ever closer to the sun. As the wax holding his wings together began to melt, Icarus felt the feathers come loose, and he plummeted from the sky, his joyful cries turning to screams of terror as he fell into the sea below. Despite Daedalus' desperate attempts to save him, Icarus drowned in the churning waves.

Heartbroken by the loss of his son, Daedalus continued his flight alone, his heart heavy with grief and regret. Eventually, he reached the safety of the island of Sicily, where he sought refuge and solace from the pain of his loss. There, amid the rugged cliffs and windswept shores, Daedalus mourned the death of Icarus, his tears mingling with the salt spray of the sea. Yet even in his darkest hour, he found solace in his craft, dedicating himself to the pursuit of art and invention as a way to honor the memory of his beloved son.

This detailed retelling of Daedalus' story provides a richer understanding of his character and the events that shaped his fate. It explores themes of ambition, hubris, and the bonds of family, offering a timeless lesson in the dangers of pride and the consequences of disobedience.

Atalanta

Atalanta is a prominent figure in Greek mythology, known for her exceptional speed and skill in hunting. Her story is quite fascinating.

Birth and Exile: Atalanta was the daughter of King Iasus of Arcadia. However, shortly after her birth, her father abandoned her on a mountaintop because he had wanted a son. She was then found and raised by a she-bear and later by hunters who took her in. As she grew up, Atalanta became a skilled huntress, renowned for her speed and prowess with the bow and arrow. She swore an oath of virginity to the goddess Artemis, dedicating herself to a life of hunting and remaining unmarried.

The Calydonian Boar Hunt: King Oeneus of Calydon had forgotten to honor Artemis with offerings, so the goddess sent a gigantic boar to ravage the land. Meleager, a hero, gathered a band of famous hunters, including Atalanta, to kill the boar. During the hunt, Atalanta proved her skills by inflicting the first wound on the beast, contributing significantly to its demise.

The Golden Fleece: Atalanta's most famous tale revolves around her participation in the hunt for the Golden Fleece. Jason, the leader of the Argonauts, sought the Golden Fleece as part of his quest. Atalanta joined the crew of the ship Argo, becoming the only female Argonaut. During the journey, she displayed her bravery and abilities numerous times, proving herself equal to her male companions.

Atalanta's story is often interpreted as a symbol of female empowerment and independence in Greek mythology. Despite the patriarchal society in which she lived, Atalanta refused to conform to traditional gender roles and instead pursued her own path as a skilled warrior and hunter.

Jason

There are several stories about individuals named **Jason** throughout history and mythology. One of the most famous is Jason from Greek mythology, particularly known for his quest for the Golden Fleece. Here's a brief summary:

Jason was the son of King Aeson of Iolcus, but he was raised by the centaur Chiron after his uncle Pelias seized the throne and threatened his life. When Jason reached adulthood, he returned to claim his rightful throne. Pelias, fearing a prophecy that a man wearing one sandal would be his downfall, sent Jason on a seemingly impossible quest to retrieve the Golden Fleece from distant Colchis.

Jason assembled a group of legendary heroes, known as the Argonauts, including Hercules, Theseus, and Orpheus, among others, to accompany him on his journey. They set sail aboard the ship Argo, hence their collective name, the Argonauts.

Their journey was perilous and filled with many challenges, including encounters with monsters like the Harpies, the Clashing Rocks, and the dragon guarding the Golden Fleece. Along the way, Jason met and fell in love with Medea, the daughter of the King of Colchis, who possessed powerful magical abilities.

With Medea's help, Jason succeeded in obtaining the Golden Fleece. However, their troubles were far from over. Medea had betrayed her family to aid Jason, and they faced the wrath of her father, King Aeëtes. Fleeing Colchis, Jason and Medea encountered numerous trials on their journey back to Greece.

Upon their return to Iolcus, Jason faced more challenges, including dealing with the treacherous Pelias. With Medea's assistance once again, Jason orchestrated the downfall of Pelias and reclaimed his throne.

Despite their triumphs, Jason's story took a tragic turn. His relationship with Medea soured, and he eventually abandoned her for another woman. In retaliation, Medea killed Jason's new wife and their children before fleeing to Athens, leaving Jason devastated and alone.

Jason's tale is a classic example of heroism, betrayal, and the consequences of one's actions in Greek mythology.

Otrera

Otrera the legendary queen who, according to some accounts, was the mother of Queen Hippolyta and the founder of the Amazons in Greek mythology. Here's a summary of her story:

Birth and Rule: Queen Otrera was said to be a daughter of Ares, the Greek god of war, making her a sister to Hippolyta, Penthesilea, and other figures associated with the Amazons. She was renowned for her strength, courage, and leadership abilities.

According to some accounts, Otrera was the one who organized and led the Amazons in their earliest days. She was credited with establishing their society as a matriarchal warrior culture, where women held positions of power and authority.

Otrera was said to have been a skilled warrior and a wise leader, who led her tribe in battles against various enemies. She was often depicted as a symbol of female empowerment and independence in Greek mythology.

While Queen Otrera's story is not as widely known as that of her daughter Hippolyta or her sister Penthesilea, she is an important figure in Amazonian mythology and has been featured in various myths, legends, and works of art throughout history. She represents the strength, resilience, and leadership of women in ancient Greek culture.

Phaethon

Phaethon was a lesser, but still interesting, figure from Greek mythology. Here's a summary of his story:

Phaethon was the son of the Sun god Helios and a mortal woman named Clymene. Despite being raised by his mother, Phaethon yearned to prove his divine lineage and sought confirmation from his father of the nature of his birth.

To reassure Phaethon of his parentage, Helios granted him one wish. Overwhelmed with pride and ambition, Phaethon requested to drive his father's chariot across the sky for a day. Helios reluctantly agreed, but warned his son of the dangers and the difficulty of controlling the fiery chariot.

Despite his father's warnings, Phaethon eagerly took the reins of the sun chariot. However, he quickly lost control of the powerful horses and veered off course, scorching the earth and endangering all life below.

The gods, witnessing the chaos caused by Phaethon's reckless actions, intervened to prevent further destruction. Zeus, the king of the gods, struck Phaethon down with a thunderbolt, sending him plummeting from the sky.

Phaethon's fall resulted in his death, and his charred remains were scattered across the heavens. Some versions of the myth state that his grieving sisters, the Heliades, were transformed into poplar trees, and their tears became amber as they wept for their brother.

The story of Phaethon serves as a cautionary tale about the dangers of hubris and the consequences of overreaching ambition. It highlights the importance of humility and respect for the power of the gods in Greek mythology.

Orpheus

The story of **Orpheus** is one of the most famous myths in Greek mythology. Orpheus was a legendary musician and poet, known for his incredible skill with the lyre, a stringed instrument resembling a small harp. Here's his tale:

Orpheus was the son of the god Apollo and the muse Calliope. From a young age, he showed exceptional talent in music and poetry.

His music was so beautiful that it could charm wild beasts, calm raging seas, and even make rocks and trees dance.

Orpheus fell deeply in love with a beautiful nymph named Eurydice, and they soon married. However, their happiness was short-lived. Shortly after their wedding, tragedy struck. While fleeing from a lustful god named Aristaeus, god of beekeeping and cheese making. Eurydice was bitten by a venomous snake and died.

Devastated by the loss of his beloved wife, Orpheus decided to journey to the underworld to try to bring her back. Armed only with his lyre and his voice, he descended into the realm of Hades, the god of the underworld.

Once in the underworld, Orpheus played his lyre and sang with such sorrowful beauty that even the souls of the dead were moved to tears. Hades and Persephone, the rulers of the underworld, were so moved by his music that they agreed to grant Orpheus's request on one condition: he must lead Eurydice out of the underworld without looking back until they reached the surface.

Orpheus eagerly agreed and began the journey back to the land of the living, with Eurydice following behind him. As they ascended, Orpheus was tormented by doubt and fear. Unable to resist the urge to see if Eurydice was truly behind him, he glanced back just before they reached the surface.

In that moment, Eurydice was whisked back into the underworld, forever lost to Orpheus. Heartbroken and filled with grief, Orpheus wandered the earth, playing mournful melodies that echoed his sorrow. Eventually, he was torn apart by the followers of Dionysus, the god of wine, in a fit of jealousy.

The story of Orpheus serves as a cautionary tale about the power of love, loss, and the consequences of disobeying the gods' commands.

It also highlights the enduring power of music and art to express the deepest emotions of the human soul.

Psyche

The story of **Psyche**, is a beautiful, but heartbreaking, part of Greek mythology.

Psyche was a mortal woman renowned for her extraordinary beauty, so much so that she drew comparisons to the goddess Aphrodite, the goddess of love and beauty herself. However, this beauty became a source of trouble as people began to neglect the worship of Aphrodite, instead offering their devotion to Psyche.

Enraged, Aphrodite sought to punish Psyche. She ordered her son, Eros (also known as Cupid), the god of love, to make Psyche fall in love with the most hideous creature he could find. However, when Eros saw Psyche, he was so struck by her beauty that he accidentally pricked himself with his own arrow and fell deeply in love with her.

Unable to carry out his mother's orders, Eros instead arranged for Psyche to be taken to a magnificent palace, where he visited her only at night, keeping his identity hidden in the darkness. Psyche lived a luxurious life in the palace but was never allowed to see her mysterious husband.

Despite her happiness, Psyche grew curious about her husband's true identity. With the encouragement of her jealous sisters, she devised a plan to uncover the truth. One night, she lit a lamp to see her husband's face while he slept. To her astonishment, she discovered that her husband was none other than Eros, the god of love.

In her excitement, Psyche accidentally spilled hot oil from the lamp onto Eros, waking him. Shocked and hurt by her betrayal, Eros fled from Psyche, leaving her alone and heartbroken.

Psyche, deeply regretful of her actions, embarked on a series of trials and tasks to prove her love and win back Eros. With the help of various gods and creatures, she completed each challenge, demonstrating her unwavering devotion to Eros.

Eventually, Psyche's perseverance moved the gods, and they allowed her to reunite with Eros. In a grand ceremony, Psyche was granted immortality and became the goddess of the soul, joining Eros in eternal love.

The story of Psyche and Eros is often interpreted as an allegory for the journey of the soul towards enlightenment and the power of love to overcome obstacles. It highlights themes of curiosity, trust, perseverance, and the transformative nature of love in Greek mythology. It was also the beginning for the story: "Beauty and the Beast".

Chapter 5

The Famous Monsters

As we learned when we read about the famous heroes of Greek Mythology, the stories of the Ancient Greeks were filled with monsters of many shapes and sizes. Some of the monsters were enemies to be fought, but others were the servants or even friends of the Gods.

Here are some of the most well known Greek Monsters:

Hydra: In the marshes of Lerna, there dwelled a fearsome creature known as the Hydra, a multi-headed serpent with regenerative powers. For every head Heracles severed, two more grew in its place. It was a daunting task as part of his Twelve Labors to defeat this beast. With the help of his nephew Iolaus, Heracles devised a strategy. As he cleaved each head, Iolaus cauterized the stump, preventing regrowth. In the end, Heracles emerged victorious, slaying the Hydra and completing one of his greatest challenges.

Cerberus: Guarding the entrance to the Underworld stood Cerberus, the monstrous three-headed dog with a serpent's tail. No mortal dared to approach the realm of Hades while Cerberus stood watch. However, during his Twelve Labors, Heracles descended into the Underworld to capture Cerberus as part of his trials. With sheer strength and cunning, Heracles wrestled Cerberus into submission and brought him to the surface, where the beast reluctantly obeyed his command.

Cyclops: The Cyclops were formidable one-eyed giants known for their brute strength and craftsmanship. Among them was Polyphemus, son of Poseidon, who encountered the cunning Odysseus and his crew. Polyphemus trapped them in his cave, intending to devour them one by one. However, Odysseus devised a plan to blind the Cyclops by driving a sharpened stake into his eye while he slept. In agony, Polyphemus called upon his father for revenge, but Odysseus and his crew narrowly escaped, leaving the blinded giant raging in his cave.

Scylla: In the treacherous waters opposite Charybdis lurked Scylla, a sea monster with multiple heads and a serpent's body. Sailors feared her as she snatched them from their ships with her razor-sharp teeth. Scylla was once a beautiful nymph transformed by the jealous sorceress Circe. She took residence in a cliffside cave, terrorizing sailors who dared to pass through the strait. Many brave souls fell victim to her voracious appetite before navigating the perilous waters.

Charybdis: Across from the deadly Scylla lay Charybdis, a massive whirlpool monster capable of swallowing entire ships. Three times a day, she would inhale the sea, creating a vortex that threatened to devour everything in its path. Sailors navigated the strait with caution, fearing the wrath of Charybdis. Only the most skilled seafarers could outmaneuver her grasp, avoiding the fate of being swallowed whole by the relentless whirlpool.

Centaurs: Half-human, half-horse creatures, the Centaurs were notorious for their wild and drunken behavior. They roamed the forests and mountains, often engaging in raucous revelry. Their association with Dionysus, the god of wine and ecstasy, further fueled their hedonistic lifestyle. However, their antics sometimes led to conflicts with mortals and other creatures, resulting in chaotic and violent encounters.

Satyr: Satyrs, half-man, half-goat beings, were companions of Dionysus, embodying the wild and untamed aspects of nature. They were known for their love of wine, music, and revelry, often joining the god in his ecstatic celebrations. Satyrs were mischievous and lustful, pursuing nymphs and engaging in playful antics in the forests and mountains where they roamed.

Arachne: Arachne, a mortal weaver of exceptional skill, challenged the goddess Athena to a weaving contest out of pride and hubris. Despite Athena's warnings, Arachne boasted of her talent, proclaiming herself superior to the goddess. In response, Athena accepted the challenge, weaving a tapestry depicting the glory of the gods. Arachne, however, wove a tapestry mocking the deities' flaws and scandals. Enraged by her insolence, Athena transformed Arachne into a spider, condemning her to weave for eternity.

Typhon: Typhon, the monstrous giant with a hundred dragon heads and a body covered in serpents, instilled fear in both gods and mortals. Born from the primordial forces of Chaos and Gaia, Typhon sought to overthrow the Olympian gods and reign supreme. In a cataclysmic battle, Typhon clashed with Zeus, hurling mountains and unleashing storms upon the earth. However, Zeus emerged victorious, casting Typhon into the depths of Tartarus, where he remained imprisoned beneath the weight of Mount Etna, his fiery breath still causing tremors and eruptions to this day.

Medusa: Medusa was originally a priestess of Athena, the goddess of wisdom and warfare. However, she caught the eye of Poseidon, the god of the sea, and the two of them ended up together in Athena's temple. Enraged by their desecration, Athena punished Medusa by turning her into a hideous monster. Medusa was banished to a remote island, where she lived in solitude, turning anyone who ventured near into stone with her gaze. It was said that the only way to defeat her was to look at her reflection in a mirror, as the reflection would turn her to stone instead.

Chapter 6

The Minor Gods

We've talked about the most famous and busy of the Ancient Greek Gods, Heroes, and Monsters, but there are a few more that deserve a mention. Maybe in another book we can dive into the details of their stories, but here's are a few of the most well known minor gods.

Aeolus: Aeolus, the god of the winds, was entrusted by the gods to maintain order among the tumultuous forces of nature. He resided on the floating island of Aeolia, where he kept the winds locked away in a vast cave. When Odysseus visited Aeolia during his journey home from Troy, Aeolus graciously provided him with a gift: a bag containing all the winds except the favorable west wind to hasten his return. Odysseus was cautioned to only open the bag a bit at a time, but driven by curiosity and mistrust, Odysseus' crew opened the bag, releasing a tempest that blew them off course, prolonging their journey.

Eros: Eros, the mischievous god of love, was often depicted as a winged youth armed with bow and arrows. His arrows had the power to incite love and desire in the hearts of gods and mortals alike. Eros himself fell victim to his own arrows when he fell deeply in love with Psyche, a mortal woman. Their tumultuous romance, marked by trials and tribulations, eventually led to their union and immortalization in the hearts of lovers everywhere.

Hebe: Hebe, the goddess of youth, was the daughter of Zeus and Hera, revered for her eternal youth and beauty. She served as the cupbearer of the gods, pouring nectar at their feasts on Mount Olympus. Hebe's marriage to the hero Heracles granted him immortality, as he ascended to the realm of the gods upon his death. Her presence symbolized the eternal vitality and rejuvenation that youth brings to both mortals and immortals alike.

Nike: Nike, the goddess of victory, was celebrated for her role in granting triumph to those who emerged victorious in battle, sports, and contests of all kinds. She was often depicted with wings, carrying a laurel wreath to crown the victors. Nike's presence symbolized the attainment of glory and achievement, inspiring warriors and athletes to strive for excellence and success in their endeavors.

Pan: Pan, the rustic god of the wild, shepherds, and flocks, roamed the forests and mountains, playing his reed pipes and cavorting with nymphs. He was depicted as a satyr, a half-man, half-goat creature with horns and a shaggy beard, embodying the untamed forces of nature. Pan's boisterous revelry and joyful music brought merriment to all who encountered him, inspiring a sense of wild abandon and connection to the natural world.

Nemesis: Nemesis, the implacable goddess of retribution and revenge, ensured that mortals received their just desserts for their hubris and transgressions. She was often depicted as a winged goddess wielding a whip or a sword, delivering divine justice to those who succumbed to arrogance and overreach. Nemesis' role served as a cautionary tale, reminding mortals of the consequences of their actions and the inevitability of accountability.

Iris: Iris, the radiant goddess of the rainbow and messenger of the gods, traversed the heavens on her multicolored arc, delivering divine messages and announcements to gods and mortals alike. She was revered for her swiftness and grace, serving as a bridge between the mortal realm and the divine. Iris' appearance signaled the onset of rainbows and showers, symbolizing the renewal and promise of life after the storm.

Hypnos: Hypnos, the gentle god of sleep, dwelled in the realm of dreams, lulling gods and mortals alike into peaceful slumber. He was depicted as a winged youth carrying a poppy, whose soporific effects induced rest and relaxation. Hypnos' tranquil embrace provided respite from the cares and worries of the waking world, offering solace and rejuvenation to those in need of rest.

Thanatos: Thanatos, the somber god of death, presided over the final passage of souls from the mortal realm to the afterlife. Often depicted as a winged figure bearing a sword or an extinguished torch, he embodied the inevitability of mortality and the cessation of life. Thanatos' presence served as a reminder of the transient nature of existence, prompting mortals to cherish the time they had and to live their lives with purpose and meaning.

Eris: Eris, (not to be confused with Eros) the goddess of strife and discord, was infamous for her role in causing chaos and discord among the gods and mortals. She was best known for her involvement in the events leading up to the Trojan War. Angered by not being invited to the wedding of Peleus and Thetis, Eris tossed a golden apple inscribed with the words "For the Fairest" among the guests. This sparked a rivalry among the goddesses Hera, Athena, and Aphrodite, ultimately leading to the Judgment of Paris and the subsequent Trojan War.

Morpheus: Morpheus, the god of dreams, held sway over the realm of sleep, shaping the dreams of gods and mortals alike. He was one of the sons of Hypnos, the god of sleep, and was often depicted as a winged figure carrying a horn filled with dreams. Morpheus could assume any form in dreams, allowing him to convey messages and visions to those who slumbered. His domain provided a realm of escape and imagination, where dreams held the power to inspire, frighten, and enlighten.

Persephone: Persephone, the goddess of springtime and queen of the Underworld, was the daughter of Zeus and Demeter, the goddess of agriculture. Her abduction by Hades, the god of the Underworld, led to her becoming queen of the realm of the dead. Persephone's annual descent into the Underworld marked the onset of winter, while her return to the world above heralded the arrival of spring. She was revered as a symbol of rebirth and renewal, embodying the cyclical nature of life and death.

Asclepius: Asclepius, the god of medicine and healing, was the son of Apollo and the mortal princess Coronis. He was revered as a skilled physician and healer, capable of curing ailments and injuries that baffled mortal doctors. Asclepius' knowledge of medicine was so great that he could even restore the dead to life. However, his ability to cheat death angered Zeus, who struck him down with a thunderbolt. In death, Asclepius was immortalized as a constellation in the night sky, forever watching over those in need of healing.

Helios: Helios, the god of the sun, drove his chariot across the sky each day, bringing light and warmth to the world below. He was depicted as a radiant figure crowned with the sun's rays, guiding his fiery steeds across the heavens. Helios' journey marked the passage of time, from dawn to dusk, illuminating the earth with his golden light. He was revered as a powerful and benevolent deity, whose presence brought life and vitality to all living beings. Though in some myths Apollo was the god of the sun.

Selene: Selene, the goddess of the moon, rode her silver chariot across the night sky, bathing the world in her gentle moonlight. She was often depicted as a luminous figure with a crescent moon adorning her brow, guiding the tides and illuminating the darkness. Selene's ethereal beauty and serenity captivated mortals, inspiring poets and lovers alike. She was revered as a symbol of mystery and enchantment, casting her spell over the nocturnal realm. In some myths Artemis is depicted as the moon goddess.

Moros: Moros, the god of impending doom, was one of the primordial deities who emerged from Chaos at the dawn of creation. He presided over the fateful moments when destiny was sealed and events were set into motion. Moros' presence was felt in times of crisis and upheaval, signaling the inevitable march of fate towards its inexorable conclusion. He was both feared and respected as the harbinger of endings and beginnings, reminding mortals of the impermanence of all things.

Oizys: Oizys, the goddess of misery and anxiety, was the daughter of Nyx, the goddess of night. She embodied the dark and oppressive aspects of existence, bringing sorrow and despair to those who crossed her path. Oizys was often depicted as a mournful figure veiled in shadows, whispering her melancholy lamentations to those in distress. Her presence served as a reminder of the fragility of happiness and the inevitability of suffering in the mortal realm.

Lethe: Lethe, the goddess of forgetfulness and oblivion, presided over the river of forgetfulness in the Underworld. She was one of the five rivers that flowed through the realm of Hades, erasing the memories of the souls who drank from its waters. Lethe's embrace offered solace to the departed, freeing them from the burdens of their past lives and allowing them to find peace in the afterlife. Her presence symbolized the release from earthly cares and the eternal rest that awaited the souls of the dead.

Pheme: Pheme, the goddess of fame, gossip, and rumor, was the personification of spoken words and whispers. She was often depicted as a winged figure bearing a trumpet, spreading news and tales across the mortal realm. Pheme's words could either elevate individuals to greatness or tarnish their reputations with scandal and gossip. She was both revered and feared for her ability to shape public opinion and influence the course of events with her words.

Lyssa: Lyssa, the goddess of madness and rage, was the personification of unbridled fury and insanity. She was often invoked in moments of extreme emotional distress or when seeking vengeance against one's enemies. Lyssa's presence could drive mortals to acts of violence and destruction, unleashing their innermost demons upon the world. She was both feared and revered for her power to incite chaos and mayhem, leaving devastation in her wake.

Geras: Geras, the god of old age, was the personification of the physical and mental decline that accompanies the passage of time. He was often depicted as a feeble old man leaning on a crutch, symbolizing the frailty and vulnerability of old age. Geras' presence served as a reminder of mortality's inevitability, prompting mortals to cherish the fleeting moments of youth and vitality before succumbing to the ravages of time.

Momus: Momus, the god of satire, mockery, and criticism, was known for his sharp wit and caustic humor. He was often depicted as a cynical figure with a perpetual scowl, ridiculing the flaws and shortcomings of gods and mortals alike. Momus' biting commentary spared no one, exposing the hypocrisy and absurdity of the world around him. Despite his penchant for stirring up trouble, Momus' critiques often served as a catalyst for change and self-reflection.

Apate: Apate, the goddess of deceit and deception, was the personification of cunning and treachery. She was often invoked by those seeking to deceive others or to conceal their true intentions. Apate's influence could sow discord and mistrust among friends and allies, undermining the bonds of trust and cooperation that held communities together. She was both feared and reviled for her ability to manipulate and manipulate the hearts and minds of mortals.

The Horae: The Horae, the goddesses of the seasons and the natural portions of time, were the daughters of Zeus and Themis, the goddess of divine law and order. They were responsible for maintaining the orderly progression of the seasons and overseeing the passage of time. The Horae were depicted as graceful maidens adorned with flowers and fruits, symbolizing the cyclical nature of life and the eternal renewal of the natural world.

The Muses: The Muses, the goddesses of inspiration in literature, science, and the arts, were the daughters of Zeus and Mnemosyne, the goddess of memory. They presided over the realms of poetry, music, dance, history, and astronomy, inspiring mortals to create works of beauty and excellence. The Muses were often depicted as nine sisters dancing and singing in harmony, their voices and melodies echoing across the heavens and inspiring all who heard them.

The Charites (Graces): The Charites, also known as the Graces, were the goddesses of charm, beauty, and creativity. They were the daughters of Zeus and Eurynome, the daughter of Oceanus, and were associated with the pleasures of life and the celebration of beauty in all its forms. The Charites were often depicted as three sisters adorned with flowers and garlands, radiating joy and grace wherever they went. Their presence brought harmony and elegance to the world, inspiring mortals to embrace the finer things in life.

The Moirai (Fates): The Moirai, also known as the Fates, were the goddesses of fate and destiny, responsible for weaving the threads of mortal lives and determining their ultimate outcome. They were three sisters: Clotho, who spun the thread of life; Lachesis, who measured the thread's length; and Atropos, who cut the thread when it was time for a mortal to die. The Moirai were revered as impartial arbiters of fate, whose decisions could not be swayed by gods or mortals alike.

The Erinyes (Furies): The Erinyes, also known as the Furies, were the goddesses of vengeance, tasked with punishing those who had committed heinous crimes or broken sacred oaths. They were born from the blood of Uranus when he was castrated by his son Cronus, and they embodied the primal forces of retribution and justice. The Erinyes were often depicted as fierce, winged women armed with whips and torches, relentlessly pursuing their targets until justice was served.

The Anemoi: The Anemoi were the gods of the four winds, each associated with a cardinal direction and possessing unique character-istics. They were Boreas (north wind), Zephyrus (west wind), Notus (south wind), and Eurus (east wind). The Anemoi were depicted as winged figures or as powerful horses driving chariots across the sky, bringing rain, storms, or gentle breezes depending on their mood and temperament. They were revered as both benefactors and harbingers of change, shaping the weather and influencing the course of events in the mortal realm.

The Astra Planeti: The Astra Planeti were the gods of the wan-dering stars, known as the planets in the night sky. They were as-sociated with various aspects of life and were believed to influence the destinies of mortals. The Astra Planeti included Mercury, Venus, Mars, Jupiter, and Saturn, each with their own unique attributes and powers. They were revered as celestial beings, guiding the course of events in the mortal realm and embodying the forces of fate and destiny.

The Nymphs: The Nymphs were minor goddesses of nature, often associated with specific locations such as forests, rivers, mountains, and meadows. They were depicted as beautiful young women, embodying the vitality and spirit of the natural world. The Nymphs were revered as guardians of the wilderness, nurturing the flora and fauna that inhabited their domains. They were often sought after by mortals for their beauty and companionship, but they could also be capricious and elusive, vanishing into the wilds when pursued.

Aristaeus: Aristaeus, the god of beekeeping and cheese making, was a minor deity associated with agriculture and rural life. He was the son of Apollo and the nymph Cyrene, and he was revered as a patron of shepherds, beekeepers, and farmers. Aristaeus was credited with inventing the art of beekeeping and teaching humans the secrets of cheese making. He was often depicted as a youthful figure tending to his beehives and herds, embodying the pastoral virtues of hard work and ingenuity.

Proteus: Proteus, the god of sea change, rivers, and transformation, was a prophetic old man who dwelled in the depths of the sea. He was revered as a shape-shifter who could assume any form he desired, making him difficult to capture or control. Proteus was sought after by mortals seeking knowledge of the future, but he could only be compelled to reveal his secrets through cunning and guile. He was both revered as a wise and ancient deity and feared as a harbinger of change and uncertainty.

Triton: Triton, the god of the sea, was the son of Poseidon and Amphitrite, the rulers of the ocean. He was depicted as a merman with the upper body of a human and the lower body of a fish, often carrying a conch shell trumpet. Triton was revered as the messenger of the sea, announcing the arrival of his father Poseidon with blasts from his trumpet. He was also associated with the calm and tumultuous aspects of the sea, guiding sailors through treacherous waters and calming stormy seas with his soothing melodies.

Thalassa: Thalassa, the primordial goddess of the sea, was one of the first beings to emerge from Chaos at the dawn of creation. She embodied the vast and boundless expanse of the ocean, nurturing life within her depths and shaping the world with her gentle currents. Thalassa was revered as a maternal figure, providing sustenance and shelter to all creatures that inhabited the sea. She was often depicted as a serene and serene woman, surrounded by the waves and accompanied by a retinue of sea creatures.

Pontus: Pontus, the primordial god of the sea, was the son of Gaia, the earth goddess, and the father of the sea deities. He embodied the raw power and primal forces of the ocean, ruling over its depths and commanding its vast legions of creatures. Pontus was revered as a formidable and ancient deity, whose presence inspired both awe and reverence among gods and mortals alike. He was often depicted as a mighty figure rising from the waves, his voice booming like thunder and his trident striking fear into the hearts of all who beheld him.

Tartarus: Tartarus, the primordial god of the deepest part of the underworld, was a dark and shadowy realm reserved for the most wicked and malevolent souls. He was one of the first beings to emerge from Chaos at the dawn of creation, embodying the boundless depths of the abyss. Tartarus was revered as a fearsome and implacable deity, whose realm served as a prison for the Titans and other ancient enemies of the gods. He was often depicted as a vast and yawning chasm, swallowing up all who dared to defy the will of the gods.

Ananke: Ananke, the goddess of necessity, fate, and compulsion, was one of the first beings to emerge from Chaos at the dawn of creation. She embodied the inexorable forces that governed the cosmos, guiding the destinies of gods and mortals alike. Ananke was revered as a powerful and implacable deity, whose decrees could not be defied or evaded. She was often depicted as a veiled figure with a stern and unyielding gaze, holding the cosmic spindle upon which the threads of fate were spun.

Hemera: Hemera, the goddess of daylight, was the daughter of Erebus, the god of darkness, and Nyx, the goddess of night. She embodied the radiant splendor of the sun, illuminating the world with her golden rays and dispelling the shadows of the night. Hemera was revered as a bringer of life and vitality, whose presence heralded the onset of a new day and the promise of renewal. She was often depicted as a radiant figure riding across the sky in her chariot, casting light and warmth upon the earth below.

Nyx: Nyx, the goddess of night, was one of the first beings to emerge from Chaos at the dawn of creation. She embodied the primordial darkness that enveloped the cosmos, shrouding the world in mystery and shadow. Nyx was revered as a powerful and enigmatic deity, whose presence inspired awe and fear among gods and mortals alike. She was often depicted as a veiled figure cloaked in darkness, her starry mantle twinkling with the light of distant galaxies.

Charon: Charon, the ferryman of the dead, was tasked with guiding souls across the river Styx to the realm of the dead. He was often depicted as a somber figure robed in tattered garments, wielding an oar to steer his ferryboat through the murky waters of the underworld. Charon demanded payment in the form of a coin placed upon the eyes or mouth of the deceased, ensuring safe passage to the afterlife. He was both feared and respected by the spirits of the departed, who relied on him to transport them to their final resting place.

Panacea: Panacea, the goddess of universal remedy and healing, was revered as a bringer of health and wellness to those in need. She was often depicted as a gentle figure carrying a basket of medicinal herbs, offering relief from pain and suffering to all who sought her aid. Panacea's healing touch could cure diseases and ailments that baffled mortal physicians, restoring vitality and vigor to the sick and infirm. She was revered as a symbol of hope and compassion, whose presence brought comfort and solace to the afflicted.

Adrestia: Adrestia, the goddess of revolt, just retribution, and balance between good and evil, was revered as a bringer of justice and equality to the mortal realm. She was often depicted as a stern figure wielding a sword and a set of scales, symbolizing her role as a judge and arbiter of righteousness. Adrestia's presence inspired courage and righteousness in those who fought against injustice and oppression, ensuring that the scales of justice were always kept in balance. She was revered as a champion of the downtrodden and a protector of the innocent, whose wrath could be unleashed upon those who defied her will.

Aether: Aether, the god of the upper atmosphere and celestial light, was one of the primordial deities who emerged from Chaos at the dawn of creation. He embodied the radiant splendor of the heavens, illuminating the cosmos with his ethereal light. Aether was revered as a divine and transcendent deity, whose presence inspired awe and reverence among gods and mortals alike. He was often depicted as a radiant figure surrounded by a shimmering aura of light, his celestial presence casting a divine glow upon the world below.

Aidos: Aidos, the goddess of modesty, respect, and humility, was revered as a paragon of virtue and integrity. She embodied the noble qualities of self-restraint and humility, guiding mortals to act with dignity and decorum in their interactions with others. Aidos was often depicted as a veiled figure with downcast eyes, her modest demeanor serving as a reminder of the importance of humility and restraint in the pursuit of excellence. She was revered as a guardian of moral integrity and a protector of virtuous behavior, whose presence inspired reverence and respect among gods and mortals alike.

Achelous: Achelous, the god of the Achelous River, was often depicted as a river god with the upper body of a man and the lower body of a serpent or fish. He was revered as the personification of the mighty river that flowed through the countryside, providing sustenance and fertility to the land. Achelous was also associated with the transformative power of water, which could shape the landscape and carve out new paths through the earth. He was often invoked by farmers and fishermen seeking his blessings for bountiful harvests and abundant catches.

Palaemon: Palaemon, the god of the sea and harbors, was often associated with protection during voyages and maritime expeditions. He was revered as a guardian of sailors and fishermen, ensuring safe passage across the treacherous waters of the sea. Palaemon was also associated with the bounty of the ocean, providing sustenance and livelihoods to those who depended on its riches. He was often depicted as a youthful figure riding upon a dolphin or guiding ships through stormy seas, his presence bringing comfort and reassurance to those who sailed under his protection.

Enyo: Enyo, the goddess of war and destruction, was a fierce and formidable deity revered for her prowess in battle. She was often depicted as a fierce warrior wielding a spear or a sword, leading armies into battle and instilling fear in the hearts of her enemies. Enyo was associated with the chaotic and destructive aspects of war, inspiring bloodlust and violence in those who invoked her name. She was both feared and revered as a relentless force of destruction, whose wrath could lay waste to entire cities and civilizations.

Hecate: Hecate, the goddess of magic, witchcraft, and ghosts, held sway over the realms of the earth, sea, and sky. She was often depicted as a triple-headed goddess with the ability to see into the past, present, and future, guiding mortals through the mysteries of life and death. Hecate was revered as a powerful and enigmatic deity, whose presence was both feared and respected by gods and mortals alike. She was often invoked by witches and sorcerers seeking her guidance and protection, as well as by those embarking on journeys or facing important decisions at crossroads.

Hymenaios: Hymenaios, the god of marriage ceremonies and weddings, was revered as a bringer of joy and union to lovers and couples. He was often invoked by those seeking his blessing for their nuptials, ensuring that their marriages would be blessed with happiness and prosperity. Hymenaios was associated with the festive and celebratory aspects of weddings, presiding over the rituals and ceremonies that united couples in matrimony. He was often depicted as a youthful figure adorned with flowers and garlands, his presence bringing warmth and affection to the hearts of all who witnessed his blessings.

Eileithyia: Eileithyia, the goddess of childbirth and midwifery, was revered as a protector of women in labor and a bringer of safe deliveries. She was often invoked by expectant mothers seeking her aid and guidance during childbirth, ensuring that their deliveries would be smooth and successful. Eileithyia was associated with the transformative power of childbirth, which brought new life into the world and ensured the continuity of the human race. She was often depicted as a gentle and nurturing figure, comforting and reassuring mothers-to-be as they brought forth new life into the world.

Panacea: Panacea, the goddess of healing and universal remedy, was revered as a bringer of health and wellness to those in need. She was often depicted as a gentle figure carrying a basket of medicinal herbs, offering relief from pain and suffering to all who sought her aid. Panacea's healing touch could cure diseases and ailments that baffled mortal physicians, restoring vitality and vigor to the sick and infirm. She was revered as a symbol of hope and compassion, whose presence brought comfort and solace to the afflicted.

Bia: Bia, the goddess of force, power, and might, was revered as a bringer of strength and victory to those who called upon her aid. She was often invoked by warriors seeking her blessings before battle, ensuring that their arms would be strong and their hearts resolute in the face of adversity. Bia was associated with the raw and primal forces of nature, embodying the fierce and indomitable spirit of conquest and triumph. She was often depicted as a formidable figure wielding a sword or a shield, her presence inspiring awe and reverence among gods and mortals alike.

Harmonia: Harmonia, the goddess of harmony and concord, was revered as a bringer of peace and unity to those who sought her guidance. She was often invoked by rulers and diplomats seeking to resolve conflicts and establish treaties between nations. Harmonia was associated with the harmonious balance of opposing forces, ensuring that discord and strife were kept in check and that cooperation and understanding prevailed. She was often depicted as a serene and tranquil figure, her presence bringing calm and serenity to the hearts of all who beheld her.

Herakles (Hercules): Herakles, the god of heroes, was one of the most celebrated heroes of Greek mythology, renowned for his strength, courage, and noble deeds. He was the son of Zeus and Alcmene, a mortal woman, and was gifted with extraordinary abilities from birth. Herakles' legendary exploits included the Twelve Labors, a series of impossible tasks assigned to him by King Eurystheus as punishment for killing his wife and children in a fit of madness. Despite facing numerous trials and challenges, Herakles emerged victorious in all his labors, earning him the admiration and respect of gods and mortals alike. He was revered as a paragon of heroism and virtue, whose name would be remembered and celebrated for generations to come.

Psyche: Psyche, the goddess of the mortal soul, was a mortal woman whose beauty and grace rivaled that of the goddess Aphrodite. She was the daughter of a king, who, in his pride, proclaimed her to be more beautiful than Aphrodite herself. Enraged by this insult, Aphrodite sought to punish Psyche by ordering her son Eros to make her fall in love with the vilest creature in the world. However, Eros was so captivated by Psyche's beauty that he fell in love with her himself. Despite facing numerous trials and tribulations, including a journey to the underworld, Psyche ultimately proved herself worthy of divine love and was granted immortality, ascending to the realm of the gods to live with Eros forever.

Voluptas: Voluptas, the goddess of pleasure and delight, was revered as a bringer of joy and indulgence to those who sought her company. She was often depicted as a youthful figure adorned with flowers and jewels, her presence inspiring feelings of warmth and contentment in those who beheld her. Voluptas was associated with the pleasures of the senses, including feasting, music, and lovemaking, and she was often invoked by revelers seeking to indulge in earthly delights. She was revered as a symbol of hedonism and excess, whose presence brought merriment and revelry to all who embraced her.

Conclusion

Well, you're done. You've read of lots of crazy and cool myths. We didn't cover all of them. That would be a crazy big book and this is just our first step!

But I hope you found some stories that you liked and can see how these myths continually show up in other stories and even television and movies.

My personal favorite is the story of Percyus.

I hope that this guide expands your mind.

Join me in my other books. What they are? You'll have to wait and find out.

About the author

Hi, I'm Trapper Stocks.

I've always loved writing, finding a way to tell a story, and I'm very excited to be publishing this book.

Special thanks to Rick Riordan for writing the Percy Jackson series, which really got me into Greek mythology, my aunt who published this book, and again to my amazing friends Hadlee, Sullivan, and Sam.

Made in the USA
Coppell, TX
04 September 2024